Written By: Sally Zolkosky Labadie

Illustrated By: "Jeremiah"

Halo ●●●●
Publishing International

For more information about the author:
Sally Zolkosky Labadie
Email: labadie.sally@gmail.com

Library of Congress Control Number: 2011917544
ISBN 978-1-61244-029-3

Halo
Publishing International
www.halopublishing.com

Printed in the United States of America

To Ed, who brought Wooster home and into my life.

-Sally

Wooster was Sarina's little rooster. He had silver gray and black feathers that shone in the sun, and tiny feathers on his feet, like all banty cochins. He lived in a little hutch in the garage, but Sarina left his door open when she was outside working so he could get some exercise.

Wooster loved to walk in the grass and hunt for bugs to eat. He followed Sarina into a hay field so she could help him find grasshoppers.

He ran behind Sarina when she went into the house, and flew onto the back of a kitchen chair. "No, Wooster. This is not where you eat," said Sarina. Laughingly, she put him back outside.

On special days Sarina took Wooster to school. He hopped into the car and sat beside her all the way to school. The children in her classroom enjoyed taking him outside at recess. Wooster followed them around, hoping they would find bugs for him to eat.

Wooster loved to ride in the car to the post office and even to the veterinarian's office. He flew onto Sarina's arm and went into the buildings with her. He squawked softly for Dr. Linda.

One nice, sunny day Wooster was scratching in the grass for bugs when Sarina went into the house. He saw her car sitting in the driveway with the windows open. He flew through the window and onto the seat.

"Now," he thought, "how do I start this thing? I'd like to go to school!"

He jumped onto the gear shift. It moved.

He jumped onto the steering wheel. The car started rolling towards the garage.

"ER ER ER AWK!" he squawked, "That's the wrong way!"

The car slowly rolled into the garage and stopped when it bumped into the back wall. Wooster jumped out the window and ran as fast as he could. He was so frightened that he kept running down the sidewalk and turned onto the main street of town.

He ran to Dr. Linda's office and jumped up at the door, over and over again, to get someone's attention.

Dr. Linda heard something at the door and went to see what it was. When she opened it, Wooster ran in and jumped onto the counter.

"Wooster!" she exclaimed as she hugged the little rooster. "What are you doing here? Your little heart is beating so fast. Is something the matter?" She looked outside. Sarina wasn't around. "I'd better call Sarina to come and get you."

Sarina was surprised to hear that Wooster was at Dr. Linda's office. She said she would be right there to get him. She walked to get the car, and saw it was in the garage. "I thought I left the car in the driveway," she said out loud. "I must be getting forgetful."

"Wooster!" She exclaimed as she picked him up off the counter in the office. "What happened? How did you get here?" But all Wooster could say was, "ER ER ER AWK!"

When Sarina mowed the grass, Wooster ran after the mower, squawking as loudly as he could. Sarina stopped, and Wooster jumped onto her lap. He rode while she cut the grass.

"This is great fun," he thought.

Wooster rode with her, his feathers flapping in the breeze. She stopped the mower near the creek that was at the back of her yard. She got off, and put Wooster on the seat. "Wait here," she said, as she disappeared around some bushes to pick up sticks that could get caught in the mower.

"I don't want to wait," he said to himself. "I've watched her do this a lot. I can drive it myself." He jumped onto the gearshift, and it dropped into drive. The mower started rolling, right toward the creek. Wooster hopped onto the steering wheel and tried to turn it away from the water.

"Oh, no," he said frantically in his squawking way. The mower headed right down into the creek, where it stopped suddenly, its nose in the water. Wooster was thrown off —SPLASH! —Right into the water! "ER ER ER AWK!" he squawked.

He flapped his wings and splashed while he climbed clumsily out of the water. Chickens aren't supposed to swim!

He looked around for Sarina and saw her walking back towards the mower. Wooster ran as fast as his little legs could go for the safety of his little hutch so he could dry out. He didn't want her to see him all wet.

Sarina found the mower in the water, and wondered how it got there. "I left Wooster on it," she said. "No, it couldn't be! But could he—? And where is he?"

Wooster sat on the top of his hutch drying his feathers. He hoped Sarina didn't see how wet he was. He decided he was better off being a pet chicken than driving cars and lawn mowers —at least for the rest of that day.

CPSIA information can be obtained
at www.ICGtesting.com
Printed in the USA
LVIW011705081212

310733LV00002B